MOG
and
Bunny
and
Other Stories

MOG

and
Bunny
and
Other Stories

written and illustrated by

Judith Kerr

HarperCollins *Children's Books*

First published in paperback in Great Britain
by HarperCollins Children's Books in 2013

10 9 8 7 6 5 4 3 2

ISBN: 978-0-00-752808-0

HarperCollins Children's Books is a division of HarperCollins Publishers Ltd.
Text and illustrations copyright © Kerr-Kneale Productions Ltd 1988, 1996, 1995.
The author / illustrator asserts the moral right to be identified as the author / illustrator of the work.
A CIP catalogue record for this book is available from the British Library. All rights reserved.
No part of this publication may be reproduced, stored in a retrieval system, or transmitted
in any form or by any means, electronic, mechanical, photocopying, recording or otherwise,
without the prior permission of HarperCollins Publishers Ltd, 77-85 Fulham Palace Road,
Hammersmith, London W6 8JB.

Visit our website at www.harpercollins.co.uk

Printed and bound in China

Contents

MOG
and Bunny

For Lucy and Alexander

One day Mog got a present.
"Here you are, Mog," said Nicky.
"This is for you. It's called Bunny."

Mog liked Bunny.

She carried him about.

She played with him…

and played with him…

and played…

and played…

and played with him.

He was her best thing.

When Mog came to have her supper,
Bunny came too.

Sometimes Mog thought
Bunny would like a drink.

But Bunny wasn't very good at drinking.
"Oh dear," said Debbie. "Look where
Bunny's got to."

And she put him on the radiator to dry.

At night Bunny slept with Mog in her basket.

During the day, when Mog was busy,
she always put Bunny somewhere nice.
You never knew where Bunny would get to.

Sometimes Bunny liked to be quiet and cosy,

and sometimes he liked to be where there was a lot going on.

Mr and Mrs Thomas didn't understand this.
They didn't say, "Look where Bunny's got to."
They shouted, "Yukk!"

They yelled, "Arrgh! What a horrible, dirty thing!"

And they threatened
to throw Bunny away
in the dustbin.

One day Mr Thomas said,
"Let's have supper in the garden."

Everyone helped to carry things out of the house.

It was a lovely supper.

But suddenly…

...there was a crash of thunder and it poured with rain.

"Quick! Inside!" shouted Mrs Thomas. "It's bedtime anyway."

"Where's Mog?"
said Debbie.
"I expect she's keeping
dry under a bush,"
said Mrs Thomas.
"She'll come in later."

In the middle of the night,
Debbie and Nicky
woke up. Mog
hadn't come
in and it was
still pouring
with rain.

"Let's go and find her," said Debbie.

It was very dark in the garden.
They shouted, "Mog! Where are you, Mog?"
But nothing happened.

Then they heard a meow.
"There she is!" shouted
Nicky. "Come on, Mog!
Come inside!"
But Mog just went
on sitting in
the rain.

It was...

dripping...

off her nose.

"What's the matter, Mog?" said Debbie.
Then she said, "Oh dear! Look where Bunny's got to."

Nicky picked Bunny up
and showed him to Mog.
"It's all right, Mog," he said.
"We've set Bunny free.
You can come inside now."

Then they carried Bunny through the dark garden...

and through the house...

and they put him on the radiator to dry.

Then they all had a big sleep.

In the morning they told Mrs Thomas
what had happened, and how Mog had
stayed with Bunny in the dark and the rain.

Debbie said, "You won't really throw
Bunny away in the dustbin, will you?"
Mrs Thomas said, "No, never. It would
make Mog too sad."

Then she sighed and said, "Perhaps Bunny is not
quite so horrible, now he's been washed by the rain."
They all looked on the radiator.

But this is where Bunny had got to.

MOG
and the V.E.T.

For Susannah Thraves

One day Mog was trying to catch a butterfly.
She jumped high in the air. She jumped and jumped.
Suddenly something happened to her paw.
It was very sore.

She smelled it. It was still sore.

Then she licked it, but it was still sore.

She tried to walk on it, but it was very, very sore.

Mog thought, "I've got three other paws.
I'll just walk on them instead."

"What's the matter with Mog?" said Nicky.
Debbie said, "I think she's got a sore paw."
"Poor Mog," said Mr Thomas. "Let me see."
But Mog wouldn't let anyone see her paw.
It was too sore.

"Oh dear," said Mrs Thomas. "If it's no better tomorrow she'll have to go to the vee ee tee." She said vee ee tee instead of vet so that Mog wouldn't understand.
Mog hated going to the vet, but Mrs Thomas thought she probably couldn't spell.

That evening Mog did not want to eat
her supper because her paw was too sore.
It was so sore that she couldn't sleep.

In the morning, she did not eat her breakfast.
She just lay on the floor feeling sad.

Suddenly she was not on the floor anymore.
Mrs Thomas had picked her up.
Mog thought, "What's happening? It's rude
to pick me up without asking me first."

Then she was in a basket.
But it was not her proper basket.
It was a nasty basket that shut her in.
Mog did not like that basket.
She meowed a big meow.

Debbie said, "It's all right, Mog.
We're taking you to have your paw made better."
But Mog just wanted to get out of the basket.

Then they were in the car. It made a big noise and all
the houses and trees and people rushed past outside.
Mog knew that was not right. She meowed and meowed.

At last the houses
stopped rushing past
and suddenly Mog
was in a room.

It was a room with lots of other animals.
Mog thought, "I knew it! I knew it! This is the
place I hate!" And she meowed more than ever.

The other animals were
sitting quietly with their people.
They were surprised to hear Mog
make so much noise.

"It's all right, Mog," said Debbie.
"It's all right, Mog," said Nicky.
"It's all right, puss," said the nurse.
But Mog wouldn't stop meowing.
After a while the other animals thought
perhaps Mog knew something they didn't.

The dogs began to bark.

The parrot began to squawk.

Even the hamster
said "Eek! Eek!"

They made so much noise
that the vet came to see
what was happening.
"Oh, it's Mog," said the vet.
"I thought it might be.
Perhaps I'd better see her first."

Mog suddenly thought she liked the shut-in basket after all.
The vet tried to look at her, but it was very difficult.

"Perhaps this way will be easier," said the vet.

"There," said the vet at last.
"Now, let's have a look at that paw."

He did something very quickly.
Then he said, "All done.
She had a nasty thorn in her paw,
and look – here it is!"

"Now I'll just give her a little pill and...

…Ow!" said the vet.
"Oh Mog!" said Debbie.
"I'm so sorry," said Mrs Thomas.
"Watch out for that cat!"
shouted the vet.
"Quick! Catch it!" shouted
the nurse.

"I'll catch it,"
thought a big dog.
"And I'll catch it too,"
thought a little dog.
"But I'll catch it first,"
thought a third dog.

"Heel!" "Sit!" "Stay!" "Come back!"
shouted the dogs' people.
But the dogs took no notice.

"They're all going wild!" shouted the nurse.
The hamster got mixed up in the wild rush.
The vet got mixed up in it too.

"Stop! We can't have animals going wild," said the vet.
The dogs' people all shouted, "Heel!" "Sit!" "Stay!" and
"Come back!" again and after a while the dogs stopped.

"Come on, Mog," said Nicky. "You're a very silly cat."
"Back into your basket," said Debbie.

"Goodbye," said the vet. "I think she'll be all better
in the morning after a good night's sleep."

And that night Mog did have a good sleep.

But the vet did not have
a good sleep.

The vet had a dream. It was a dream about wild animals.

Mog had a dream too, but it was a lovely dream.
Mog dreamt that she was a butterfly.

And in the morning her paw was no longer sore.
It was not sore when she licked it.
It was not sore when she walked on it.
It was not sore when she jumped up high.
She was better. She was all better.
She was totally, completely better.

And the vet was almost better too.

MOG
and the Granny

For Eve and Thomas
and their Granny and Grandpa

One day Mog was waiting for Debbie
to come home from school.
Mog always knew when Debbie was coming.
She didn't know how she knew. She just knew.
Suddenly a picture would come into her head
of Debbie coming down the road.
Then she would go to meet her.
Debbie said, "School's all finished for
the summer, Mog. Isn't it exciting!"
Mog said nothing. She didn't like things
to be exciting. She liked them to be the same.

Inside the house
everyone was excited too.
Mrs Thomas was packing.

Mr Thomas
was looking
for something
important.

Nicky was dancing
and singing a song
he had made up.

"We're going to America where the skyscrapers are.
We're not going by train but on an aeroplane.
We'll see all the sights,
and it will be very
surprising because
they have their
days when we
have our
nights!"

Debbie said, "You can't come, Mog.
But you're going to a nice granny's house.
She'll look after you till we come back."

Next day Mog went to the granny's house.
The granny was old with very thin legs.
First Mog thought she had three legs.
Then she saw that one of them was a stick.
Debbie said, "Goodbye, dear Mog."
The granny said, "I'll look after Mog.
And she'll have my Tibbles for company."
Mog thought, "Tibbles? Nobody told me
that there would be another cat.
At least he sounds quite small."

Tibbles had been small to start with but then he had grown. "Here's a little friend for you," said the granny.

Tibbles liked surprising people.

And he liked Mog's basket. The granny said, "Don't be silly, Tibbles. Let Mog have her basket, and you can sleep on my bed."

Mog sat in her basket, but she couldn't sleep.
She thought of her house. She thought of Debbie.
Suddenly a picture of Debbie came into her head.
Debbie was in a high place and there were even
higher places all round. It was all too high.
Mog didn't think Debbie should be there.

"Whatever is the matter, Mog?" said the granny.

"You'd better come and snuggle up with us."

A few days later the postman brought a card.
"It's from Debbie," said the granny.
"She's been to the top of a skyscraper."

Mog thought the card smelled of Debbie.

Tibbles didn't have a card.
He had tea in a saucer instead.
He was very fond of tea.

Tibbles had an open window instead of a cat flap.
He had a yard to play in.

Sometimes Mog and Tibbles played together.

Sometimes they chased each other.

Sometimes they liked each other

and sometimes they didn't.

The granny gave them nice food to eat.
She went to the shops to buy it.
They always had the same, but they
always thought the other one's was nicer.

The first time the granny went shopping, Mog had a big surprise.
The granny no longer had a stick. She had wheels instead.

She gave Tibbles a ride.

"What about you, Mog?" said the granny.
But Mog thought the wheels were too surprising.

One day the granny put out her best tea cups.
She said, "We're going to have a party."
It was very hot, so they had the party in the yard.

A lot of other grannies came. They were surprised to see Mog.
The granny told them about Mog's people. She said,
"They've been all over America and now they're ending up
at a special Red Indian show."

The grannies stayed a long time.
Mog got very tired.
She thought of Debbie and
she wondered what Red Indians were.

Suddenly a picture of Debbie came into her head.
Debbie was smiling at a big bird.
Mog knew it was a bird because it had feathers.
But it had a face like a person. It was a person bird.
And there were more person birds nearby.
Why was Debbie smiling? Those big person birds
might fly away with her and hurt her.

Mog wanted to save Debbie.
She did a big jump.
Tibbles liked tea inside him, not outside.
"Oh dear," said the granny.

"Oh dear," said all the other grannies.
"And your best cup too." Then they went home.

That night Mog did not
sleep in the granny's bed.
She was too sad.

She was still sad in the morning.
She thought of Tibbles and
the granny being upset.
She thought of Debbie
and the person birds.

Suddenly a picture of Debbie came into her head.
The person birds had not hurt her at all.
Instead they had given her some of their feathers
and a baby person bird as a present. She was
smiling and excited, and she was coming home.
Mog thought, "I must be there to meet her."

She ran out of the yard

and across a road

and down another road

…and up a tree.

After a time the dog went home.
Mog wanted to go home too,
but she couldn't get down the tree.

She tried this way

and that way,

but she was stuck,
and it was getting late,
and Debbie would
be coming home.

Mog thought, "There's nobody to help me."
But there was somebody.

"Quick, Mog! Jump!" said the granny,
and Mog jumped.

"We'll have to get a move on," said the granny.

"We haven't much time," said the granny.

"I think we can just make it," said the granny.

AND THEY DID!
When Debbie got home, Mog was there to meet her.

"We've never had such excitement," said the granny.
"Mog will have to come and stay with Tibbles again."

Mog said nothing.
She didn't like things to be exciting.
She liked them to be the same.

Judith Kerr was born in Berlin, but her family left Germany in 1933 to escape the rising Nazi party, and came to England. She studied at the Central School of Art and later worked as a scriptwriter for the BBC.

Judith married the celebrated screenwriter Nigel Kneale in 1954. She left the BBC to look after their two children, who inspired her first picture book, *The Tiger Who Came to Tea*. Published in 1968, it has been in print for over forty years and has become a much-loved classic.

Judith was awarded an OBE for her services to children's literature and holocaust education in 2012, and continues to write and illustrate children's books from her home in London.

A selection of bestselling picture books by Judith Kerr

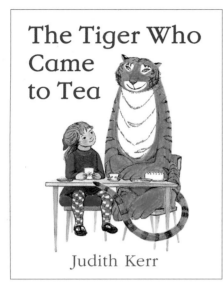

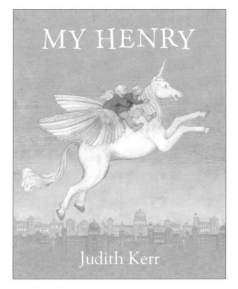

The Tiger Who Came to Tea
'A modern classic'
Independent

My Henry
'For all the depth of underlying emotion there's a celebratory feel to it' *Telegraph*

The Great Granny Gang
'Kerr is at the height of her powers' *Sunday Times*

Also look out for

Mog the Forgetful Cat
Mog's Christmas
Mog and the Baby
Mog in the Dark
Mog and the Amazing Birthday Caper
Mog on Fox Night
Mog's Bad Thing
Goodbye Mog
When Willy Went to the Wedding
How Mrs Monkey Missed the Ark
Birdie Halleluyah!
The Other Goose
Goose in a Hole
Twinkles, Arthur and Puss
One Night in the Zoo

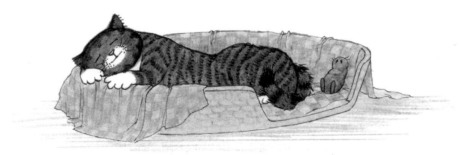